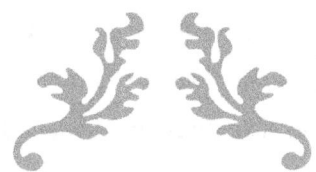

HA'PENNY JENNY

The Fairies Saga

DANI HAVILAND

Ha'penny Jenny and *The Fairies Saga* are works of fiction. Names, places, characters, and incidents are the product of the author's imagination or used fictitiously for the reader's entertainment. Any resemblance to persons living, dead, or fictional, events, business establishments, or locales, is entirely coincidental.

Copyright 2014 by Dani Haviland
Published by Chill Out!
ISBN 978-0-6922178-7-0
All rights reserved

BOOKS IN THE SERIES:

Part One: NAKED IN THE WINTER WIND (previously released as three books: AMNESIA, ABANDONED, ADOPTIONS)

Part One and a half: HA'PENNY JENNY (novella)

Part Two: AYE, I AM A FAIRY

Part Three: DANCES NAKED

Part Four: THE GREAT BIG FAIRY

Part Five: FAIRIES DOWN UNDER

SOMETHING SPECIAL:

Just so you won't get confused about who's who, I put a cast of characters on the last page of this book. I figured it was the easiest place to refer to. And if while reading, you find that someone is narrating the story—that it's in the first person—that's just Evie taking over. Sometimes that old lady in a young person's body just won't shush!

Contents

1 History of Jenny

August 6, 1781

Master Simon may have been the person who physically put the painkillers and antibiotics in the pockets of the pink terrycloth robe I wore from the 21st century back to 1781, but I knew it was God guiding his hands.

"Thank You, Lord," I said, as I downed half an oxycodone.

I didn't like the idea of taking *any* pain medication, but this was for the purpose intended, not for getting high, and was only half a dose. The musket ball had pierced muscle and bone close to my heart, only three days ago. Sarah said the surgeon and surgical nurse were sure to have scrubbed aggressively and that I had both internal and external stitches. The jostling wagon ride home—stretching at all those tender parts—added to the reasons my pain was so great.

I didn't like to admit to myself or anyone else that I needed the chemical help, but the pain was so great, I couldn't focus and could barely function. Dulling the pain with whisky wasn't an option I was willing to take. It would take a substantial amount to work, anyhow. I didn't want my judgment impaired, and besides, I was nursing. I didn't want Jody's 160 proof to pass through my milk to the babies. Sarah insisted that half a pain pill wouldn't bother them.

I was a tough old broad in a young woman's body, and my pain threshold was pretty high, but by all rights, I should still be in a hospital bed, letting others take care of me. Or at the very least, I should be kicked back on my little couch, letting my family take care of my chores and tend to my three babies.

But I was too proud for that. I felt obligated to at least see to the limited tasks my dear sweet husband and good mother-in-law allowed me to perform—feeding my six-week-old babies and changing their clouts. My range of motion was restricted because of the pain. On top of that, I noticed that I was downright cranky if I didn't get at least some relief. Sarah didn't have a problem with me taking the pills—no one did, for that matter—but I felt guilty that I couldn't handle day-to-day tasks without taking 'substances.'

"This isn't like labor," Sarah reminded me. "You did wonderful with that, beyond wonderful. You were perfect as far as how well you handled the contractions, but this is different. With labor, you got a few minutes of relief, more or less, between the pains. This is constant discomfort. Take the pills. I'll make sure you don't take too many, and that I always have willow bark tea brewed to rotate with the painkillers. Eventually you won't need either one of them. All right?"

"Okay, but I still feel like a failure." I accepted the cup of water, swallowed half a pill, and then realized something. "Hey, just think how much whisky I'm saving! Me taking a pill now and then is better than everyone drinking in order to put up with how crabby I get when I'm hurting, huh?"

Jody had walked in unobserved and responded, "Nah, we'd jest ignore ye either way. We'd drink whether ye were cranky or no." He gave me a fatherly kiss on the top of my head. "Are ye feelin' better today, lass?"

"Yes, much better than yesterday, thank you. You know what I'd like to do—and this may sound crazy—but I want to go outside in the sunshine. I know it's hot, but, well, I guess my body needs it. Vitamin D, right, Sarah?"

"That's true. Speaking of nutrition, there's still one banana left. Do you want it now or later?"

"Where's Jenny? I'll share it with her," I said. "She sure is a good helper."

My adopted pre-adolescent daughter had become my extra set of arms. She even offered to feed me. "No, but thank you for the offer." I saw her face fall. "But when these three start on porritch, I'll definitely need your help," then watched her beam at the prospect.

Just then, Jenny, the lady of the moment, ran through the door, her bounty clutched in her arms. "Look what I got! Daddy said I could pick them, and he even let me use his knife to cut them off so I didn't tear up the plant by pulling on 'em. They're peppers, he said, and José says if you fix them right, they're real good with cheese and eggs, and since we already have those, maybe I can help make dinner tonight. Grannie, do you know how to cook these?" she asked, as she pivoted in place, looking for an empty flat spot to set her harvest.

"Uh, no…" Sarah drew out her answer, then looked at me. "Maybe your mother does."

I almost purred at being called mother again, then felt weepy, and it wasn't because of the presence of what looked like Anaheim green chilies. I was that happy. "Yes, I know a great way to fix them: chiles rellenos." Now my eyes were definitely tearing, but for another reason. "Jenny, put them into that basket, please. Then, would you like to share the last banana with me?"

"Ooh! Ooh! You mean the yellow custard fruit? There's still one left? Are you sure you don't want the whole thing? I mean, Grannie says you have to eat lots of food because your body is making milk to feed all those babies, but if you think there's enough for both of us, yes, yes, yes, I want some, too!" Jenny was literally jumping up and down with excitement.

"Well, while your siblings are quiet, let's go outside for a little walk and talk. I want to know more about my big girl." I nodded to Sarah to make sure she was fine with watching—or rather, listening for—the babies.

"You two go ahead and take those peppers out there with you. I don't have enough room in here as it is."

"Sure, Grannnie!" Jenny trilled.

I cut off the end of the banana, wiped the blade, and put Sarah's paring knife back on the table. I had given Wallace my Leatherman, sort of as a wedding gift. He had always admired it, although I never felt like he coveted it.

"When I get to feeling better, and have more time, maybe I can make a little holster for it," I had told him.

"Well, I'm not too sure how I'd wear a holster, but I can make a little pouch to put it in so it's handy. You know, on second thought, I think I may just have to make a sporran. I'm sure Jody would let me use his as a pattern. He seems to be able to keep everything he needs in there."

Jenny started in on a new subject, breaking my reverie. "So I'm your big girl now? Does that mean that I'm your oldest daughter?" she asked with a mouthful of banana.

"It's not nice to speak with food in your mouth, dear," I said, hoping the subject would change. I didn't want to tell her that she wasn't my eldest. That would be too confusing for her and painful for me. I still missed Leah, the daughter I had left behind in the 21st century.

"But I am your biggest daughter, huh?" she persisted, making sure she had swallowed her food before she spoke.

I rolled my eyes comically and said, "Well, you're the biggest one I see. Now, how old are you?" I asked, redirecting our discussion.

"Uh, I dunno," she practically whispered, her face red in embarrassment. She became unusually quiet, and focused on her bare foot as she made circles in the dirt with her big toe. Her energy level was nil and her happiness in the negative zone.

"Ooh! Ooh!" I squealed, mimicking her animated, attention-getting noises. She looked up and smiled at me, genuinely happy to see me acting like her. "Does that mean I get to pick your birthday? I mean, the year and everything?" I was dipping up and down, as if ready to jump. I would have, too, but was afraid the jostling would hurt my shoulder.

"Yeah! Yeah! You and Daddy can pick my birthday, even the year! Should I have the same birthday as Wren and Judah and Leo, or maybe it can be on Christmas or…or…"

Jenny was all wound up, dancing around what I called the family tree, blabbering names of events like Easter that she could share a birthday with.

"Slow down there. First off, Easter wouldn't work because it falls on a different date every year. It has something to do with spring equinox and full moons and Sundays and…" I looked over and saw that I had lost her. "Anyway," I continued, "I want you to have your very own day. But it would be nice to have it in the spring, so when you *do* go to school, your classmates can celebrate with you. We can make a birthday cake and give you a party and…"

I looked down and saw that Jenny was crying. "What's wrong, honey?" I gathered her close. I really had no idea what was wrong. One moody female in the house—me—was already one too many.

"I'm just so happy," she sobbed. "I get to go to school *and* have a party? And a cake? Just for me?" Her upturned faced was searching mine, asking for confirmation that what I had just told her was true.

"Yes, but I'll have to find out if there's a school around here. I don't know if there is one yet. But," I stressed, "if there isn't one, we'll just have to start one ourselves. In the meantime, I'll make sure we set aside a little time…uh…five days a week. I'll teach you to read and write and do your numbers. You can take time off from schooling on Saturdays and Sundays."

"I know what Sunday is," she bragged. "I learned about it from Mrs. Short. She kinda took me in as a helper when my brothers and me—that is, my other brothers that died and went to heaven—when we went into town to do some tradin' and get some supplies. She was real nice sometimes, but other times…" Jenny shook her head back and forth, as if she was having a hard time believing what she was thinking, "She was *real* mean."

"Do you want to talk about it?" I looked at the last of the banana, took one more bite, and then offered the rest to her.

"Thanks," she said, and bit off the last morsel. She chewed slowly, then suddenly stopped and spit the half-chewed mass into her hand. "Can we get the seeds out of this and plant them? We can have more custard fruit if we plant the seeds. Then we can have them every day!"

"No, no," I said, as I shook my head, refusing her masticated glob. "Go ahead and finish eating it. Bananas are different than most fruits. They don't grow from seeds. They grow from..." I paused, trying to figure out how to explain rhizomes and cuttings, "they grow from runners, and we don't have the main plant around here. So, just enjoy it while you have it, okay?"

"Okay. That means all right, huh?" she said, then licked off the slimy mess, bent over, and wiped her sticky hands through the fine soil at her feet. She rubbed her palms together and let the little grunge worms of food residue mixed with dirt fall onto the ground. She briskly dusted off her hands, turned them over for closer inspection, and then wiped them on the back of her skirt. She had apparently adapted to her earlier soap-less environment and found a way to keep from becoming grimy and tacky. I'd have to remember to teach her to use soap and water after her little dry cleaning routines.

"Do you still want to know about Mrs. Short?" she asked, then bit her bottom lip in mildly suppressed anticipation. She and I hadn't had much alone time, and she wanted as much of my attention as she could get.

"Sure, tell me all about her while we walk a little." My body needed exercise, at least something other than lifting or bending over babies.

"Well, she started out real nice. She saw me in town with my brothers—my other brothers..." She looked at me to make sure I understood. I nodded, so she continued. "Well, I don't think she liked that bag I was wearing for clothes. My brothers didn't have any pants 'cept the ones what they wore. For me, they just cut holes in old flour sacks for dresses. I had two of them," Jenny said proudly. "But Mrs. Short said I needed somethin' proper. I was a young lady and deserved more, whatever that meant. I mean, I didn't pay for nothin', so why did I deserve somethin'?

7

"Well, anyhow, she asked my brothers—my other brothers..." she looked up again, and I nodded again, "she asked them if it was all right if I stayed with her a while. They said they had some trappin' to do, and if she wanted, then I could stay with her for the whole winter. Well, that was all right with me 'cause it got real cold when they went out in the woods like that. They did their best to keep me warm and made me a coat outta some of the skins from the muskrats that got torn up in the traps. Those were the pelts that were spoilt and not worth much. But the coat was stiff. I couldn't move very good in it and well, when she said I could stay with her for the whole winter, and that she had a nice big fireplace, and I could sleep by the hearth and everything... Well, I asked my brothers..."

Jenny looked up at me, and before she could say 'her other brothers,' I nodded for her to proceed.

"Well, my brothers thought that it was a good idea, too. But they asked her if she could give them some bacon and flour for me since she would have me workin' for her all winter. I don't think she liked that much, but still, she gave them some.

"She was real nice at first, and I didn't have to do much. She let me sweep the floors for her and even let me put soap in a bucket with water and scrub down the hearth one day when it wasn't too cold.

"And she had this basket that she said she got from an Indian woman. It had lots of pieces of bright cloth in it. And, well, she said it was time I learned how to sew. She said her eyes weren't too good anymore, but she could still teach me what to do. So she gave me a little box and it had some needles in it. And then she showed me how to put the thread through the *eye*," Jenny looked at me to make sure she was using the right word.

8

"Yes, the eye of the needle is where the thread goes through. Go ahead. We still have some time, but I think we should head back to the porch. I didn't know I'd tire so easily."

Jenny grabbed my hand in an attempt to help me walk. It didn't make a difference as far as the walking went, but the emotional support was priceless. She was a chatterbox for sure, but she was our little chatterbox.

"So, I got to thread every one of her needles. I'm not sure how many there were, but at least ten." Jenny let go of my hand momentarily, brought up both her hands, and displayed all her fingers. "Ten," she repeated.

"See, she had me put the needle in her hand so the sharp end wouldn't hurt her, and she showed me how to do a runnin' stitch and a backstitch and a overcast stitch. Well, I guess I wasn't as fast as she thought I should be, and sometimes she'd holler at me if my stitches were too big or too messy. You see, her eyes weren't too good, but her hands could feel just fine. She'd run her fingers across my stitchin' and could tell if I messed up. If I did, she'd make me tear it all out and start all over again. That is, after she smacked my hand for bein' lazy or careless or whatever else she felt like callin' me that day.

"But she wasn't always mean. I think it was just when her head was hurtin' real bad. She had some tonic that she drank for it, and I don't know if it helped or not, but it did make her fall asleep after a while. She called it a tonic, but I think it was just whisky. I've smelt whisky before, and that's what it smelt like.

"So I sewed all sorts of bits and pieces of the cloth rags together, and then she said that since I was such a good girl—you see, she wasn't hurtin' that day—that she would help me make my own dress. She showed me how to measure myself with a piece of string,

9

and then stretch it across the cloth. Then she even let me use the shears—all by myself. Well, she said that her hands wouldn't work the shears anymore, but still, I got to use them all by myself," she repeated with pride.

"So you made your first dress all by yourself?" I asked, proud of her youthful accomplishment.

"Well, yes, I guess so. At least, I did all the cuttin' and sewin'. I made one bad cut, but she didn't even get mad at me. She said that I just had to fix it myself and learn from my mistake. Every time that I would see that bit of extra stitchin', I'd remember to measure twice and cut once. But that was the dress that I lost at the mill last week. The one that the mean man made me take off and…"

"And now you have another one, and maybe we can make you one more. And since you already know how to measure and sew, maybe you can help Grannie make one for me, too?"

I was trying to make her feel better about her talent, but I also wanted to help her forget about that vile Captain Asshole who had attacked her at the mill. Hopefully, the soldiers had taken him before whomever, and a fair judgment and punishment was ordered. Well, I knew what the punishment was supposed to be, and it wasn't up to me whether he was hanged by the neck until dead, or exiled to Elba or Timbuktu. As long as Captain Atholl MacLeod was out of our lives, that was fine by me.

2 Evie and Wallace: together at last

Sarah aimlessly fussed about in the kitchen area, intentionally avoiding eye contact with me, lifting each stack of diapers then setting it down, rearranging the cups on the shelf, shifting the chair back against the wall.

"Are you all set here for this evening? Do you have enough clean clouts, at least for tonight and tomorrow morning?" she asked.

"Yes, I'm fine, thank you." I narrowed my eyes in suspicion. "Where are you going?" There was something afoot by the tone in her voice and the attitude of her movements. She hadn't looked at me when she spoke, and that meant she was hiding something. She seemed to be investigating the room half-heartedly, but for what I didn't know.

She took a deep breath, then said a bit too casually, "Oh, Jody, Jenny, and I are going on a little trip." She kept her eyes low and brushed off a bit of transparent food or soil or whatever from her apron. "Will you and Wallace be okay by yourselves?"

"Of course, we will. He can take care of anything that I can't. And where... Oh!" I paused a moment, realization hitting me like a door slamming me in the face, "You'll be gone overnight, which means my husband and I will be here without any—shall we say?—chaperones."

Sarah blushed. She hadn't been as sly as she thought. She shrugged and said—this time looking me in the eye, "We'll just be in the barn so Wallace won't have to take care of the animals this evening or in the morning. We'll see to the feeding and such. Now, unless you yell *too loudly*, we won't disturb you, all right?"

"Well..." I said and giggled, "Don't come if Wallace yells *too loudly* either." Then I turned around and did a bit of blushing myself.

11

水

Later that evening...

"Come on, Jenny," Jody hollered, "we're gonna have a little party tonight, jest the three of us—ye, yer Grannie, and me."

"But what about Mommy and Daddy? Don't they want to come, too?"

"Well, we're gonna leave them alone tonight, aye? Sometimes a mommy and da jest need to be by themselves. Besides, I have a game I want to show ye."

"But who will help Mommy take care of the babies? She needs me, she told me so," Jenny argued, obviously hurt at not being able to stay the evening with her new siblings. "And don't Mommy and Daddy want to play the game, too?"

Sarah looked over at Jody and decided he needed a little help with the precocious little interrogator. She squatted down to Jenny's level and brushed the stray hair out of her eyes. "Well, they…um…have other things to do and really don't need our help for that. Besides, your daddy was helping Mommy with the babies before they got you. I'm sure he hasn't forgotten how to change a clout or burp a baby. Now, I have your quilt. Let's build a bed for you right over here on the clean straw. Grandpa and I will be right next to you in case you get scared."

"I don't get scared," Jenny declared strongly, and then remembered the fright at the mill last week. "Well, not much," she admitted. She looked around and saw that Grannie had already spread her quilt on the straw. "You mean we're going to be out here all night?"

"Aye, we'll have lots to do. I dinna think ye'll find it irksome." Jody opened out his fist. "See what I got fer ye."

12

Jenny peered into his huge hand. "Can I touch it?"

"Go aheid; its yers." He used the tip of his index finger to flip the bone-handled penknife onto its other side. "It's time ye had one of yer own. I'll show ye how to use it for work and…" He drew out the anticipation of the rest of his explanation by opening the folding knife and balancing it on back of his hand. "I'll show ye how to play a game, jest in case ye happen to have a spare minute or two between tendin' to yon bairns, aye?"

He quickly flipped his hand over and caught the penknife flat onto his palm. "But I think we'd best be tryin' the first few rounds with the blade shut. Jest until ye get the feel of the weight."

"Can I make arrows with it like the Indians do?" she asked, bouncing on her toes in anticipation.

"Weel, I think yer mommy would rather ye start by carvin' knittin' needles and what she calls crochet hooks. They're better tools fer a lass yer age to have."

Jenny's response of, "Hmph!" was a guttural blend of 'why?' and 'I don't think so!'

Her face changed moods several times while she studied the small-bladed instrument. "Well, I guess I can do that, but I'm gonna notch the ends of my knittin' needles and put a feather in 'em anyhow. Then maybe when I'm bigger, like next week, you can help me build a bow. I'll shoot bows and arrows at the bad Indians and keep them away for good!" she said, chest out in pride.

"Weel, the only Indians I've seen around here are the good ones, so I hope ye dinna plan on shootin' anyone. And mind ye, ye shoot the arrows, not the bows. Maybe we can build ye a target to practice yer aim so ye can knock some of those nasty crows out of the garden next month when the corn starts gettin' ripe. They always seem to be the best judges of when it's time fer the harvestin'."

3 Wedding Night

My wee three were all fed, burped, bathed, and put down to sleep. They were almost six weeks old and now looked like babies, not preemies. Their little arms and legs had filled out quickly, and their cheeks were pleasingly plump. The boys were still bigger than Wren, but she was closing the size gap quickly.

They were still too young to sleep through the night, but they stayed quiet for longer periods now. I didn't have a watch or clock, but my chest could tell time. My breasts filled at a constant rate, and if they weren't emptied at a regular interval, then I'd get uncomfortable. I knew from somewhere—probably from when Leah was a baby—that my body would adjust to more feedings during the day and fewer at night. I doubted I could last eight hours straight without nursing at least one baby, but I'd be willing to try for a four or five hour stretch of uninterrupted sleep.

"Do you need a hand with anything?" Wallace asked, as he put away the dishtowel. He had done the dishes after dinner, which left me free to give the babies their baths. They weren't 'dirty,' but a thorough rinsing freshened them up, cooled them down, and tired them out.

"No, thank you," I said, then quickly changed my mind. "On second thought, wait. I'll let you help me undress, so *I* can take a little sponge bath."

It wasn't the most romantic overture, but I didn't have much time alone with him until the next feedings. I didn't want to spend what precious little time we had alone being coy.

Wallace gulped, then grinned so wide, I thought his bottom lip would disappear altogether. He approached me slowly but decidedly, as if I was the chocolate cake he had been denied his whole life. Whoa, wait… I guess I really was like that—a real dessert, a forbidden treat—now his.

I twisted and lifted the hair off of my neck and shoulders with one hand, using the other to work the button loose on the neck of his shirt. He hadn't asked, but I was going to do a little exposing, too. "Can I see you without your shirt?" I asked.

He crossed his arms and pulled the shirt off over his head. I inhaled deeply. At last. He was mine. And we were alone. Well, alone except for our three youngest, but they were asleep.

He put his hand on each side of my gown. "May I?"

I nodded, looked up, and then gave him the same lip-disappearing smile he had given me.

He gently opened out the dress and slid it down over my shoulders, carefully lifting the left side away from my beige-colored 21st century adhesive bandage.

"It's okay; it doesn't hurt much. As long as I'm careful, we can do just about anything." I glanced up and saw that he wasn't looking at the bandaging, but my plump and perky nipples, dark brown and hard with excitement.

He caught my eye and an immediate blush rose on his cheeks. "They don't look the same without a bairn's head in front of them," he said softly.

"Hey, they're yours, too…just like the rest of me."

"Aye? Oh, aye!" His hands rose to my cheeks. "Mrs. Wallace Pomeroy-Hart, my beautiful, wise, and wonderful wife, Evie," he bent down to share the first of—hopefully—many wedding night kisses.

16

After a very thorough smooch, he whispered, "Evie. Is that short for another name?"

"Um, no." I grimaced. I didn't want to spoil the mood, but felt I needed to answer the question. "It's the name Ian gave me. I didn't know my name—or even who I was—when I found and rescued him, so he decided to call me Evie. I like the name just fine, though. It feels," I shrugged my good shoulder, "*comfortable.*"

"Hmm, I gave you the name Pomeroy-Hart when we married, but can I make a suggestion?" he asked, one eyebrow raised in hope.

"Yeah, sure," I answered, unsure of where this was going.

"Evangeline. I like the name Evangeline. We would still call you Evie, but you would be *my* Evangeline."

I felt my eyes light up. "Wow…yes…I mean, sure. I like that name! Cool. That's a gift no one can take away from me, and I'll have it as long as I live. No, wait—I'll have it even after I'm dead! At least, for as long as anyone remembers me." I was flattered with the gift of the new name and giddy at the prospect of immortality.

"Well, we'll just have to write stories so the life and times of Evangeline Pomeroy-Hart will be passed down through the ages—to our heirs, and to anyone else who's interested in life in a young America. You did say America will still be around in 200 years, right?"

"You know I did, silly. And I like the idea of a journal. I'm sure I can figure a way to get it handed down to Leah, so she can find out all about you and her siblings and the rest of her family here. I felt so bad having to leave her, but," I exhaled sharply, "I made my decision and I'm glad of it. Now, how about we seal—or would that be dedicate?—this new name with a little friction."

Wallace looked puzzled, so I helped him out with a one-armed grab around his neck, pulling him down for a long, wet kiss. "I think

17

I'd be more comfortable lying down," I suggested, and ran my hand down the side of his neck to between his pectorals.

"Oh...OH!" he exclaimed when he realized what I meant. He put his hand on mine and led me to our—well, really Jody's and Sarah's—bed.

"I've been saving it as a surprise, but," he pursed his lips and made the decision to tell me now, "I'm making a bed for us. We may not have our own home yet, but we'll have a bed for it when we do."

"Well, this will do for tonight." I snuggled into his chest and breathed in his male essence. We had only been close, physically close, a couple of times, but had never been skin to skin before. "Would you touch me, I mean, touch me all over? I've been aching for your hands... Oh, yeah..." I gasped as he began, then relaxed, and let him explore.

Wallace started at my face, air-glided his hand above my still tender shoulder, then settled his hand on my waist. He let it rest there for a moment, and used his thumb to gently stroke my belly. He brought his fingers together again, then brought them down my hips to the outside of my thighs.

"You don't have to be bashful. My body is yours, too," I said, and guided his cool fingers back over to my belly. "It's still kind of mushy from being pregnant, but it'll tighten up again."

I continued the guided tour to my intimate parts. "Right now, I'm kind of moist there because I'm so excited. It makes...um...everything go in easier," I said with a bit of embarrassment. I didn't want to be a little miss know-it-all, but I did want him to know some of the nuances that he probably had never heard about. Sarah had let it slip that Jody had a 'talk' with him. I appreciated the heads-up so I wasn't too bossy in my instructions.

18

Wallace took control from there, his bashfulness overcome by a healthy combination of curiosity and excitement.

"Mmm," I moaned as my knees parted to let him explore further.

"You're so soft down there," he said, "like a padded pillow."

I giggled, "Yeah, a furry padded pillow. I guess that's so we don't bruise our pelvic bones when we…um…"

I didn't finish with words, but decided it was time to do some of my own petting and pawing. I wrapped my hand around the shaft of his very ready cock and pulled down gently on the skin. He gasped and let out a gentle moan. "Just making sure you healed right," I said coyly.

I really was checking. I was afraid that he may have lost too much foreskin after he had been slashed in the groin area and I had to perform a little impromptu field circumcision after Pyle's Massacre last spring. I had heard horror stories about men who had been circumcised and had too much foreskin removed. It actually caused the men pain to have an erection. By the purring that Wallace was emitting, though, that wasn't the case with him.

Wallace still had his hand on my *pillow*, cradling it as if it was his prized possession. He let his thumb slip down a bit, and ever so gently touched and then rubbed just the right place. I gasped at the intense but very pleasurable sensation. I hadn't been touched there by anyone—including me—for an incredibly long time. I looked at him, swallowing hard with the excitement he had caused, and saw that he was chuckling.

"How…how…how did you know about that spot?" I stuttered.

"Oh, I got a few pointers. That one was easy to find. Now, should we see if I can find another?" He pulled his hand away and

19

started to get up on one elbow, his other arm crossing over me to assume the missionary position.

"Uh huh," I nodded. It looked like Wallace was going to take to the more intimate duties of being a husband just fine.

4 Jenny and the mumblety peg

Jenny lay on her quilt, flat on her back, pretending to be asleep. She rolled over toward Grannie and Grandpa Jody and listened. They were finally asleep. At least, they weren't whispering or giggling or telling each other to shush anymore.

Maybe if she was real quiet, they wouldn't wake up and she could go back where she belonged—to the house with Mommy and Daddy and the babies.

She had had a nice time—well, actually it was a whole heap of fun—spending the evening with Grandpa and learning how to play mumblety peg. But she missed her babies. And no matter what Grannie said, she was sure that Mommy needed her help. When the babies woke up at night with bad dreams, she was the one who rubbed their backs until they fell asleep again. It was only when they were really hungry, or had messed their clouts, or had a big burp that they were really awake. Even then, she could do everything except feed them. She needed to be there to help, so Mommy wouldn't have to work so hard and her shoulder could get better.

Jenny lifted her head and looked to make sure Grannie and Grandpa were really asleep. She couldn't see their faces, but they were very still. Only their backs were moving, in and out slowly with their breathing. Now it was safe to go back to her own bed. She tried to take her quilt, but the straw beneath it shifted when she tugged on it. She'd have to sleep without it tonight. That would be all right, though, because she only needed to sleep on top of it. She could do without it for one night. After all, she was a big girl now.

The moon was bright and lit the path to the house. She wasn't afraid of anything—not now, anyhow. All the bad men were gone, and the bears and pumas didn't come near the house, at least, not lately. Jenny looked around quickly, suddenly afraid of mountain lions, bad men, and bears, oh my!

"Eek! What are you doing up, Grandpa Jody?" she asked, twitching with embarrassment at being caught sneaking away.

"I was fixin' to ask ye the same thing. Yer supposed to be sleepin' in the barn with yer Grannie and me tonight."

Jody stood in front of her, arms across his chest like a Roman centurion, waiting for her answer.

"Um...um," she mumbled, twitching nervously. She couldn't tell him that she was sure Mommy needed her help. He had already told her at least ten times that Mommy and Daddy were fine and could do without her for one night.

"What's wrong?" he asked, noticing that she was uneasy, dancing from one foot to the other. "Do ye need to use the privy again?"

Jenny nodded frantically, then bent forward and squeezed her knees together in an exaggerated mime of urinary urgency.

"Weel, git to it. Come back to the barn as soon as yer finished. And no sneakin' back to the house, d'ye hear?"

"Yes, sir, Grandpa Jody," she said, then ran to the privy. She quickly shut the door behind her and climbed onto the seat to look through the little crescent-moon hole. She needed to make sure Grandpa was returning to the barn and wouldn't see her go back to Mommy and Daddy.

Shoot. He was still there. It looked like he was going to wait for her. Jenny decided it was time to for another tactic. "Ooh," she moaned. "Ooh! Uh, I think I'll be in here for a while, Grandpa Jody. I think I ate too many of those boiled peanuts. Ooh…" Jenny moaned and groaned dramatically for almost five minutes, or so it seemed.

"Do ye think ye can make it back to the barn by yerself? That is, when yer finished?"

Jody wasn't sure whether she really had a bellyache or not. She had eaten quite a few of the boiled peanuts, but then again, she might be trying to sneak back to the house. He'd let her be, but would listen for her. He had never told her that she shuffled her feet and made a distinctive noise when she walked. It was a good way to keep track of where she was, and—by her long, foot-dragged tracks—where she had been.

"Uh, I'll be okay. But don't wait up for me. Ooh…" Jenny put her hand to her mouth to stifle a giggle. She had fooled Grandpa Jody!

Jody walked back to the barn, stomping his feet to make sure she knew he was walking away. It looked like he was going to be on sentry duty until she decided to come out.

Ж

Jenny looked out and saw that now Grannie had come out and was talking to Grandpa Jody. His back was turned away, and it looked as if he was going to kiss Grannie again. Good! Grannie sometimes made little noises—kind of like a kitten—when he kissed her. Hopefully she would this time. Then he wouldn't hear her open the door and run to the house.

Jenny saw her grandparents were almost—no, wait, now they were—kissing. She stepped down off the privy seat and opened the door. She took two steps away and listened. Yes, they were *still* smooching. They sure liked to kiss a lot. She picked up her feet and walked on her tiptoes, being careful not to make any noise.

Just to make sure she made it to the house before they stopped kissing, she ran the last ten yards, almost stepping on the garden hoe she had forgotten to put away. Phew! Daddy was right! Someone could get hurt if the tools were left out. She'd put it away, but later, probably tomorrow. Right now, she needed to go inside and be with her babies and Mommy and Daddy.

The front door was open, but there was a blanket tacked across the middle part of the doorframe. Mommy said the cool air could come in at the bottom, and the hot air could go out the top if they hung the blanket up like that. She didn't like to sleep with the door open, but it had been too hot to bolt it shut. A big animal would make a lot of noise trying to come in, but she said it would stop if it couldn't see past the blanket. Wild critters didn't like going into the unknown.

Jenny got on her hands and knees so she could crawl under the blanket without knocking it down. Then she heard that noise. It didn't sound right. Mommy sounded like she was hurting. She was saying 'Oh, oh, oh, oh.' And Daddy was making noises, too. But she knew that noise. Kind of. It sounded like her brothers when they used to play rooster. They always made her leave, or at least cover her head with a blanket, when they did that.

Jenny cautiously threaded her neck under the quilt and saw Daddy on top of Mommy. He didn't have on any clothes and neither did she. She quickly crawled back out onto the porch, stood up, and tiptoed back toward the barn. Now she knew why they wanted to be alone. They wanted to play their own game.

"I'm okay, now," she said dejectedly as she walked up to Grandpa. He had been walking toward the privy and met her halfway.

She was sure glad she hadn't taken the shortcut back. She had fooled him—he thought that she had been in there the whole time with a bellyache. She didn't like lying to him, but she had to make sure that Mommy, Daddy, and the babies were all right.

Why didn't they just tell her that they wanted to play by themselves? She would have understood. She rolled over on top of her quilt and thought about it again. No, she would have wanted to play with them, too. But if they had just told her that they were going to play rooster, she *knew* she would have left them alone. She didn't like that game.

5 The Game of Rooster

Jody hadn't say anything when Jenny came back to the barn, but he could tell something had happened. She must have slipped out of the privy while he was talking to Sarah. How could he have let her get past him? He snorted. He knew how, but didn't want to admit to himself that he had been so engrossed in the little sexual fantasy he and Sarah were sharing—and the kiss that lasted longer than most—that Jenny had escaped the toilet and sneaked back to the house. Hopefully she hadn't see anything, but came back because she saw that nothing was going on. Hopefully, but not likely.

He had to let Wallace and Evie know that they may have had an audience last night. He should probably tell them both. It would be easier to only tell Wallace, but Evie was the one who would wind up with the chore of explaining what Jenny possibly—rather, probably—had seen.

No one knew Jenny's age, but she was old enough to know the facts of life. At least, according to Sarah she was. He had to agree with her on that one. The discomfort of giving and receiving last minute wedding night explanations that he—and then later, his son—had to go through was enough to make him swallow his conservative views on what a lad or lass should know at such an early age. It would be much easier on everyone down the road if when the time came for marriage, the newlywed had received at least a preliminary talk as a child.

Jody stomped his feet as he walked up the steps to the house, the heavy footfalls announcing his arrival. The quilt had been taken down, and the sounds and smells of a full-fare breakfast came tumbling down the boards. Hopefully, Evie had made enough for everyone, he thought, then realized how selfish he was. His stomach overrode the guilt of his covetous desire, though, and roared with greed. It didn't care if it was intruding on a wedding breakfast or not. The smell of bacon and coffee would rouse anyone's appetite.

Wallace had Leo over his shoulder and was rubbing his back. It looked as if he had just been fed and Daddy was burping him while Mommy was turning the bacon.

"I know, I know, I should be cooking outside, but I didn't want to go through the bother, and it's still early enough that the heat will dissipate," I rationalized. "Besides, I love the way it makes the house smell for the rest of the day. And I made enough for everyone, so you'd better not be mad at me, or I'll eat your share." I walked up to Jody and gave him a quick peck on the cheek. The previous night's excitement hadn't totally worn off, and I was still perky.

I pulled back and noticed that Jody was wincing as if either his collar or his shoelaces were too tight. Since he had neither, I asked, "What's wrong?" Wallace had noticed his grimace, too, and was concerned, asking with his scowl to, yes, please explain.

"I...um...think I may have failed in my task last night," Jody said. "Jenny may have sneaked over here when it was late. Ye see, she said she had a knot in her wame, and I waited fer her by the privy fer quite a while, and then I got a bit distracted..." Jody didn't know what else to say, but knew he had to try. "I dinna ask her if she came by, and she dinna offer an explanation. It was the frown she wore. She seemed what ye call mopey. I think maybe ye need to have *the talk* with the lass, Evie."

Jody hung his head in shame, let out a big sigh, then lifted his face and said, "Wallace, both of ye, I...I am so sorry."

I looked at Wallace and shrugged. "Well, if she did see something, then I can explain it. That means that *maybe*," I stressed with exaggerated exasperation, "we can have a life like the Indians do where having sex—making love—can be considered a natural part of life and not something to be hidden."

Wallace and Jody's heads snapped up, shocked at my words, but quickly returned to normal. I could tell they were both relieved. Well, at least the part where I said I'd do the investigating and explaining.

So, it turned out that all of us ate our big breakfast on the porch, the men sitting on the steps, the babies in their playpen snuggled under a light blanket, and the womenfolk sitting on chairs or benches, all of us with plates of bacon, scrambled eggs, and coffee cake balanced on our laps.

I could tell Jenny was uneasy, her head down, and nothing but a, "Yes, please," or, "No, thank you," escaping her tight lips. She had definitely seen something the night before. We could all see her reserve, but we certainly weren't going to address it at the family breakfast.

When we were done, Sarah and Jody offered to take care of the dirty dishes. Wallace looked as if he was going to say he'd help, also, but realized it would be too crowded with all three of them inside at the same time. Instead, he excused himself to the garden. "I think I'll go see how the corn is coming along. It shouldn't be too much longer and those first four rows will be ready. I've never heard of planting it in stages, but Evie was right. That small, early planting was a gamble, but we'll have roasted corn before anyone else."

That left me with two on-site caregivers for the babies, and the opportunity for a discreet facts of life talk. "Jenny, let's go for a little

28

walk," I said. "I found some raspberries, and I want you to come with me and see if they're getting ripe."

"I think the raspberries are already gone—the birds got them all," she said dejectedly. She saw my eyes shift, side-to-side, and knew that I didn't want to talk about raspberries. "But I'll go with you if you want me to," she sang out happily. She didn't have a clue about the reason for the walk, but the fact that she was going to get Mommy to herself for a few minutes didn't need an excuse.

I knew we didn't have much time. The babies still needed to be fed every couple of hours. Since I was their only source of nourishment, I couldn't be gone for too long or stray too far away. I had to cut to the chase and get the conversation started, figured out, and finalized as quickly as possible. But I also had to be both gentle and thorough.

"Jenny, did you leave the barn last night and come back to the house?" I wasn't looking her in the eye, but she was a lousy liar. I was glad of that and hoped she never learned.

"Yes, ma'am, I went to the privy," she replied with a half-truth. She also didn't know how to bluff.

"I didn't ask if you went to the privy. Did you come to the house?"

"Yes, ma'am," she answered softly, chin-to-chest, embarrassed that she had been caught.

I wanted to jump all over her for not doing as she was told, but because of the delicacy of the situation—at least, on the part that she may have seen me, her parent, engaged in sexual intercourse—I didn't want to put her on report. I bit off the 'why didn't you do as you were told!' scolding and instead asked, "What did you see?"

29

Jenny didn't answer immediately, but instead went to the raspberry bush that was picked clean of fruit. "See," she said, "the birds ate them all before we got here. If I'd lived here with you back when they were ripe, I'd 'a made sure I got them all before the birds did." She looked back at me with a smile of pride at her declaration of devotion to help provide food for her family. It faded quickly when she saw that I was still waiting for the answer to my question.

"I saw you and Daddy playing rooster," she said flatly. Then she turned the tables on me and asked accusingly, "Why didn't you just tell me you wanted to play rooster? I woulda understood and covered my head or stayed out in the barn with Grannie and Grandpa Jody. Really, I would have."

What could I say? "Rooster?" was all that escaped my lips.

"Yeah," she said slowly, "at least that's what I called it when my brothers—my other brothers, the ones that are up in heaven—used to play it. They said that I couldn't watch, and that I would have to go outside. Except in the winter when it was too cold, then they said that I could just cover my head with a blanket."

I shook my head, but didn't know what to say. She looked at me to make sure I knew what she was talking about, and then noticed that I didn't have a clue. She assumed the Mommy role and started her explanation to me—the dumbfounded child in the conversation.

"Clyde and Clayton," she said with assurance—I think she had finally decided that it was easier to call them by their given names rather than explain which brothers they were. "Well," she began anew, not sure of how to tell me, "they liked to, well, get happy together."

She looked at me and saw that I was starting to understand, at least a little. "Well, I…um…saw them playin' it outside once, and they said that I couldn't sneak up on them like that anymore. I guess they

30

did it all the time, but they said I couldn't play it with them because I was just a girl. But, then after our daddy died, that's our first daddy…"

She looked at me and saw me frown. She realized that I knew who she was talking about, so resumed. "Anyway, they said that they could play by themselves inside now since he was gone, but that I had to cover my head when they did because it wasn't for little kids or babies. Actually, they always called *me* a baby, and it made me mad because I really wasn't a baby…"

I gave her the 'look' and she stopped babbling about being called a baby. "So, they'd tell me to cover my head every once in a while at night, and then they'd make happy noises, and then one of them would 'ooh ooh ooh rah ooh!' like a rooster, so I called it the rooster game."

I breathed a deep sigh of relief. She saw that I felt better and came over and gave me a big hug around my hips. "Mommy, it's okay if you and Daddy play rooster. I'll cover my head, but please, don't make me sleep outside. I liked being with Grannie and Grandpa Jody, but I felt like you didn't love me anymore and didn't want me around."

"Oh, honey," I cooed, and bent down to wrap my arms around her shoulders. "I will always love you, and do want you around, but…" I cleared my throat and said a quick prayer for inspiration. She looked up at me, knowing that she would hear something profound. "God made mommies and daddies, and gave them *gifts* to share with each other. And," I shook my head rapidly, trying to Etch-a-Sketch erase the image of Clyde and Clayton joined with anyone, "it is not a game called rooster."

Jenny tilted her head to the side and waited for further explanation. "You see, it might look like we were doing the same thing as them," I cleared my throat, "but it's not at all alike. You know that

31

boys and girls are different; that Leo and Judah have a penis and Wren, you and me, well, we have a vagina. When you grow up and find someone you love and want to be with forever, then, Lord willing, you'll get married. And then, and *only* then will you get to share your gift. In the meantime, the vagina and penis are just used for, well, bodily functions."

"You mean like peein'?" she asked.

I didn't want to get deep into female anatomy and explain the difference between a vagina and a urethra, so simply nodded. "And you'll have changes happen in your body as you get older. You're already having some changes," I said, and pointed to her little budding breasts, "and here in a couple years, you'll get some *major* changes. But we can talk about that later. I think we still have a while before that happens and only a few more minutes before the babies start waking up. But, just so you're clear on this…"

Jenny brightened up and offered her synopsis of my mini facts of life lesson. "You and Daddy don't play rooster, but you do share your gifts, and no one else is supposed to watch. So if you want to do it, I have to go out to the barn or cover my head with a blanket."

"Well, we won't make you go out to the barn again. That was as much for you and your grandparents to have a little party of your own as it was for your Daddy and me to have…er…um…our party. But if you wake up in the middle of the night, and it looks like your Daddy and I are sharing our gifts, please, don't say anything. And yes, it would be very polite for you to cover your head and go back to sleep. Okay?"

"Okay," she replied simply, as if we had been making something big out of nothing. "Ooh, look, under here. The birds missed some berries. I'll put my hands out and you can knock 'em in."

I looked under the tangle of branches and saw the overloaded clusters. "Here, I'll put my hands underneath and you knock them down with a stick. My hands are bigger and can hold more. And I don't want you getting your hands scratched. It looks like we can have berries and cream for dessert tonight!"

6 Who did it?

"Did you do it or did Daddy do it?" Jenny asked as she peered around my elbow while I changed Wren's diaper.

"Do what?" I answered, as I continued to wipe the mustard-looking poopy mess from between the folds of the baby's vulva.

"Cut it off," she said simply.

"Oh, the little umbilicus just dries up and falls off after a week or so. See, it's still a little red, but she has a pretty little belly button. Would you hand me that cloth, please?"

I looked down at her as she placed the damp rag in my hand. There was something amiss with her. "What's wrong?"

"I didn't mean about her belly button. I mean the other thing—the peanut."

I choked back a laugh. "The penis, you mean? She's a girl and never had one. She was born like that, and you and I and Grannie were, too. Remember how I told you that boys and girls were different? Well, that's pretty much the main difference. I mean, we all have a heart and lungs." I looked down and saw that I was losing her. "We all have arms and legs and a head and eyes…" I looked at her again to make sure she was following.

Jenny was nodding her head thoughtfully. "So nobody chopped off my *penis* to make me a girl," she said, stressing the word carefully to make sure she had it right.

I nodded slowly three times, looking her in the eye to make sure she understood.

"They lied to me!" she carped, then sniffed and ran out the door, leaving me with a fistful of crappy clout and a delighted Wren, happy to be bare-assed.

7 Why did they lie to me?

I found Jenny hiding—well, sort of—by the woodpile. She was whittling something, but looked very angry, as if she were pushing her rage through the little penknife's blade into the toilet paper roll-sized piece of pine.

"What's wrong?" I almost asked if it was something I had said or done, but knew that she'd tell me the long version when she was ready.

She put her carving aside, wiped the blade on her skirt, and folded it up. Then she put the knife on the back of her right hand and flipped it over, caught it, then repeated the trick with her left hand. Grandpa Jody had showed her how to play mumblety peg only last week. It looked as if she was already pretty good at it.

She stopped showing off, and without even looking at me, asked, "Why do people lie?"

I sat down on the chopping block next to her. "Look at me, please." She did, but I wasn't sure I wanted to see *that* face. I didn't know that my sweet young girl could mix up anger and sadness so thoroughly. Shoot, I didn't know anyone could. But she was right. Why did people lie?

"I don't know for sure. I mean, it's not as if there's a book of instructions where you look up a question and the answer is right there. We have a Bible and it has many great teachings in it. It says we're not supposed to lie, but I don't know if it says *why* people lie. I guess everyone has his own reasons. I mean, if I don't know the answer to a question or a problem, I'm not afraid to say, 'I don't know,' and ask someone for help, and you shouldn't be either. But some people believe they would be admitting that they're weak—as in not as good as another person—if they don't understand. Do you understand?"

"Yes, I understand that I don't understand everything, if that's what you mean. And it's okay." Jenny gave a silly grin and wagged her head like a bobble doll. "It's okay that I don't know everything because I'm still a child."

"Yes, but I'm an adult and I'm still learning. Granny is a great healer and has been to school for many years to learn ways to mend people's bodies, but she'll be the first one to tell you that there's so much she still doesn't know…and that many times she learns from people who aren't as schooled as she is. Just because you're older or have been to more schools, doesn't make you smarter."

"So smart people lie, too?"

"Jenny, too many people lie. There have been times I've *not* told people things that I thought they didn't need to know, but I promise you, I have always tried to tell the truth." Uncertainty suddenly kicked in. "You haven't been lying, have you?"

"No. My brothers lied to me. I didn't even know what lying was for a long time. Sometimes they'd tell me one thing, like the sun always came up in the east because that's where the sun birds stayed in the mornings and it was their job to carry the sun across the sky. Other times, they said it was because the sun was a great big candle and it floated from one side of the mountains to the other and then big giants blew it out for the night. They never told me how it got back again, though, or what sun birds looked like, or where the giants slept."

Jenny's frown was back. "But when they lied to me, they made me feel like there was something wrong with me because I was a girl. They said I was born a boy, but that part got chopped off because I wasn't smart enough. That's why I had girl stuff, because my boy stuff got chopped off. Well, they called what you pee with *stuff*, but still, it's okay *not* to have a penis, isn't it?"

"Oh, good Lord, yes! Honey, *all* animals, and even some plants, have either female or male *stuff*—that is, parts. And in the case of animals, there *have* to be both males and females—like boys and girls, men and women—in order for the world to continue; that is, so new babies can be made."

Jenny still didn't look convinced. I whispered, as if sharing a secret, "Didn't you notice the boy horses were different from the girl horses?"

Jenny covered her mouth and whispered from behind her hand, "They got real big penises, huh?"

"Yes, but that's because they're big animals. And if they didn't have them, the girl horses couldn't have babies. No one chopped off the penises on half the animals in the world to make them girls." I paused, then added, "And they didn't fall off by themselves, either."

Jenny giggled. *She had put that question in Mommy's head just by thinking it real hard. Mommy had answered it without even hearing it.* She swallowed her smirk and said, "So you won't lie to me, and if I think maybe something I learned from my brothers, or maybe someone else like Mrs. Short, is wrong, I can ask you or Grannie or Daddy or Grandpa Jody about it…"

"Yes, and if none of us knows, well, then probably no one knows. Let's go back in the house and make a cake. We have enough sourdough starter for biscuits in the morning *and* cake tonight."

8 Jenny's Gold and Gems

The day was bright and sunny—but not too hot—with random breezes just strong enough to keep bugs off and sweat evaporating. Perfect for laundry. Jenny was helping me with it, but she was unusually quiet. I could feel her eyes on me. She was staring at me, but every time I tried to catch her, she'd turn away. Her energy level was also low. No one I knew had been sick, but I guess it was possible that a flu bug had hit the area.

"Is there something wrong?" I asked, and handed her a basket of clean clouts to wring out.

"What are those bumps hanging around your neck," she asked, bashfully pointing with one hand, clutching the basket close to her chest with the other.

"That's my necklace and these are gold nuggets," I said, fingering the largest one in the middle.

I hoped I didn't have to explain where it came from because I didn't remember. I had arrived in this 18th century world with a backpack, the clothes I was wearing, and a gold nugget necklace. What I didn't have was a memory of who or where I was...or when. I soon found out I was in 1780 North Carolina, but it wasn't until almost a year later that I found out I was a time traveler, that I had been born in the 20th century, and that although I seemed to be barely twenty, I had an adult daughter living in the 21st century.

"Are nuggets like dried out grapes or currants?" she asked.

"No, these are special rocks that were dug out of the ground and put on a necklace. See, feel them. They're pretty hard, but not as hard as quartz. Gold is a rare and precious metal found in the earth. It's used for currency—that is, money—for decorations, and a few other

39

things." *That was good enough for her. I certainly wasn't going to explain wiring, dental work, and the reflective coating on astronaut's visors to her!*

"Hmm, so if they make money out of gold, and gold is in rock nuggets, then maybe I can dig some out of the ground so we'll have money. Then we can buy more stuff, like a better plow for Daddy and more cloth so you and my brothers and sister can have new clothes. I'll bet I could dig for gold after all my chores were done. Would that be okay?"

Her eagerness to be allowed to help resolve our financial situation was evident in her fast blinking, sparkling eyes. That sweet and pure look of longing was priceless.

"Well, I think we'd be better off if you...well...um," I paused, hoping to find the right words to say. "I appreciate the offer," I stalled, "but I know you like to do other things like carve and crochet and..." Jenny's bottom lip was pouched out in frustration. Here she had come up with a plan of how to 'make' money, and I was trying to dissuade her. "Okay, you can dig, but how about if you start your gold mining where Daddy's planning on putting the next privy. That'll help him, and if you find any gold, you can have it all."

"Okay," she replied, jumping up and down in place, "I'll find enough to share with everybody!"

Ж

"Daddy, I want to help you dig the next privy. Mommy said I could dig for gold wherever you're going to put it since we needed a hole there anyway and it would actually help you and I want to get some gold so we can use it for money and buy you a new plow and some cloth for new clothes and maybe another pot and if I find lots of it, maybe you can buy other stuff I don't even know we need."

40

"I appreciate the help, and don't let me stop you, but gold is usually found near creeks and rivers. If you want, you can go down to our little creek and dig near the edge. But don't dig in the stream…and keep your dress clean. I don't want your mother scolding me because I let you get in the mud."

Wallace knew Jenny worked hard helping with the household chores, gardening, and watching her younger siblings, but she needed some time to herself, too. It would be nice if she had another change of clothes that she could get dirty. He never got the chance to make mud pies when he was little and would like the chance to do it with her at some point before she grew up too much. Hmph. Jenny wasn't too far from puberty, but her innocence was that of a six-year-old. He'd see if he could talk Evie into letting Jenny have a 'dirty clothes' day where she could play in the mud just before it was laundry time.

Ж

"There wasn't any gold, but look what I found," Jenny told Wren. She held up the six rocks with red stones imbedded in them. "I think they're pretty and I'm going to keep them forever and ever. I think if I use Daddy's hammer, I can knock off that gray rock around it."

Wren grabbed for the rock with the colorful bits. "No, no, you can't eat this. I have to take these to my special hiding place." Jenny put the rocks in her pocket and hoisted the baby over her shoulder. "Come on, I'll bet it's almost dinnertime."

Ж

"Lass, what can I do to turn that frown upside down?" Jody asked.

Jenny's lips pursed as she tried to figure out his riddle, then her smile grew as she realized what he was asking. "Well, you can tell me an easier way to find gold. I went to the creek, but I didn't find gold, just some pretty rocks. Is there an easier way, like when you make funny noises to call in the turkeys?"

"Well, I dinna ken of a 'gold call,' but I do ken that gold is heavy and it gets washed down creeks. That's where it's easiest to find. Ye may want to look about the edges of the rocks in the creeks, maybe even lift some of the lighter ones, and see if there's gold trapped underneath. Oh, and make sure ye check the rock on the leading side of the creek's flow. Fishin' in the creek is the easiest way I ken." He chuckled, then added, "After dinner, do ye want me to go with ye and show ye what I mean? It'll still be light out, and maybe yer da wants to go, too."

Jenny nodded rapidly, too giddy to speak. She reached over and gave Grandpa Jody a big hug. She looked up at him and sighed. She loved her mother and her Grannie whole heaps and loads, but she really did like being with the men more, especially when they were building things or figuring out how to make something work. Maybe someday, maybe next week, she could find a book that had lots of drawings in it about how things worked. Yes, she *knew* there was a book out there like that. But she'd have to wait for it.

Ж

"That was a mighty fine dinner ye made, Evie. How ye can accomplish anythin' with havin' three wee bairns about is amazin'," Jody said.

"Well, Jenny's a big help, and the garden is overflowing, so there's lots of variety. This winter might be tough, though, and the fare limited. Hmm, maybe I can figure out how to make freeze-dried meals so all I have to do is add water."

"Freeze-dried?" he asked.

42

"Actually, I don't think I'll have to freeze anything first. I can put together a food dehydrator in no time with Jenny's help," I patted Jenny on the head. "Yup, we can dry all sorts of fruits and veggies and then, hmm. I'll have to figure out a storage system and containers so they won't get dusty…"

"It's always something, isn't it?" Sarah said. "I mean, sometimes I miss having freezers and, oops." Sarah had forgotten that Jenny was in the room, and she couldn't speak of the luxuries and conveniences of the 20th and 21st centuries. "Jenny, would you refill the ewer, please?" she asked to change the subject.

Jenny grinned, said, "Yes, Grannie," and grabbed the pitcher. She didn't want them to know that she knew their secret. She didn't understand why, but she knew Grannie and Mommy weren't the same as everyone else. Mrs. Short had talked about fairies—maybe that's what they were. She didn't know what a fairy was, and Mrs. Short was having another 'headache day' when she was talking to herself about them. She had wanted to ask her about them later, when she felt better, but that's when her other brothers, Clyde and Clayton, came and took her back.

But it really didn't matter if Grannie and Mommy were fairies or not. They were her family. She loved them and they loved her. It was all right that where they lived before, they could ride in carriages that moved fast on the ground, and even faster in the air, and they had books that talked to you with pictures that moved. They were still the same people. It was just the things they had in their lives before that were different from the things they had now. Just the things.

9 The Trip to Town

"I'd like to take Jenny into town with me today. The cabinets I modified for Mr. Gibson are finished. I'd like to see if I can get a few things for us in exchange for my labor. I'd also like to get Jenny a peppermint stick. She deserves it. I doubt any parent has a child as eager to perform chores as she. "

"Sounds like a plan to me," I said.

Wallace tilted his head to the side, wordlessly asking, 'Please explain.'

I clarified, "That's a great idea. And bring back some candy for me, too." I chuckled. "I *really* don't know when the last time I had any was."

Just then, Jenny popped in, her hair freshly braided, her face spotless. She looked down at her hands, gave them a quick inspection, then presented them to me, showing off how she had washed them—with soap, this time—and had even cleaned under her fingernails.

"Looks like you're ready to go somewhere, dear. Do you have plans?"

Jenny tried to hide her grin by lowering her head, but her excitement was too great to contain. Her smile bloomed as she looked up at her father. "Do you need some help today? I mean, if you need to go somewhere, I'll come with you and help. That is, if it's okay with Mommy."

"As a matter of fact," Wallace said, drawing out the tension, "I was planning on taking the wagon into town. Would you like to come with me?"

Jenny bounced up and down on her toes, her head nodding just as fast, "Ooh, ooh, yes, yes. I want to go."

44

Wallace bent down and gave me a quick kiss. "I guess we're all set. We'll be back before dinner."

"Have fun, but stay out of trouble, you two," I said. They were so cute together. The tall and short of it. The mellow and the hyper. Who would have thought that two such diverse personalities would get along so well? Hmph. I guess the same could be said of Wallace and me. Nah! We were very different from each other, about 250 years apart in education, customs, and many experiences in general, but we complimented each other. Yin and yang, sweet and sour, tall and short. Yup, we were a perfectly balanced couple. And a very happy one, too.

Ж

It probably would have been easier for Jenny if she could have run beside the wagon rather than ridden in it. She had boundless energy and it was hard for her to sit still. "I haven't been to town in a long, loong time," she said. "Did you know that I used to live there a long— maybe even a longer—time ago?"

"I think your mother mentioned something about it to me. Did you like living in town?" When Jenny didn't answer, he looked down to make sure she had heard him. She must have. She was pondering her answer, her bottom lip stuck out in deep and confused thought. "Well, did you?" he asked again.

"I liked being warm in the winter, and the food was all right. I didn't mind working, and sometimes Mrs. Short—she was the lady who sorta bought me from my brothers, my other brothers who are in heaven..." Jenny looked up to make sure he understood. He nodded, so she continued. "Sometimes Mrs. Short was mean, but I think that was because she hurt all the time. But her son, he said some real mean things to me. I don't miss him at all!" She looked up. "I'm sure glad I have you and Mommy now. And the babies, and Grandpa Jody, and

45

Grannie, and Grandpa Julian, and José, and their pretty horses, and the goats..."

Wallace grinned as he flipped the reins, urging the sturdy draft horse along. *Just like her mother...she'd rather concentrate on the good parts of her life than the past. One of these days, the right man will come along for her. He'll be very blessed to have her as a wife. As long as he can get used to her chattiness, they'll be fine.*

Wallace hoisted the redesigned display cabinets out of the wagon and brought them into Gibson's for inspection. Jenny stayed at his elbow, her eyes wide, gawking at the inside of the store she had never been allowed to see by her former guardians.

The men were immediately busy, inspecting the workmanship and talking about angles and chamfers, shelving and drawers, so after an hour—or so it felt like to her—Jenny stepped outside to look at the town, the trees, and the cluster of buildings from a new perspective.

She wasn't a servant girl now, kept on a short rein, not allowed out of the house by the woman and her son who never let her forget that she was there as a favor, that she had to earn her meals and the right to sleep warm at night. Yes, she had a real family now, and never had to worry about a cuff to the ear or missing a meal because she talked too much, or said the wrong words. It felt good to say what was on her mind. And if she pulled an apple off a tree to eat because she was hungry, she wouldn't get smacked.

She walked to the front of the wagon, reached into her pocket, and grabbed a handful of oats for the big Belgian. Xerxes wasn't her pet—he was a work horse—but she liked to think of him as a big dog that just didn't know how to fetch or roll over. *Slurp!* But he sure could lick the treats out of her hand.

"Well, if it isn't Ha'penny Jenny," called a voice from behind the wagon.

Jenny froze. She knew that voice. And there was only one person who had ever called her that. Her eyes darted side to side. She didn't see him, but he must have seen her. *Quick! Find Daddy!*

Jenny ran toward the store, but was intercepted by the grizzled and stinky old man. "Well, if it isn't Ha'penny Jenny," he repeated with a sinister laugh. "I guess your brothers didn't want you after all, eh?"

"Da..."

Jenny's scream for her father was cut off by a grimy hand to her mouth. "Were you going to call for your daddy?" he asked. "You and I know your daddy died a long time ago. What I think is that you're here to rob the store. And then take all the goods to the devil. You're *his* child now, aren't you?"

Dick Short was back, causing trouble, but this time, his intended victim was too small to fight back.

Or so he thought.

Jenny stomped down on his foot and turned around and head-butted him in the crotch. She ran from his clutch, not paying any attention to which direction she was headed.

Dick bent over, stunned, in too much pain to even attempt to draw a breath. He fell forward onto his knees, his forehead breaking his fall. "My stuff! You broke my stuff!" he whimpered when he found his wind. He rolled over onto his side, tears falling and nose running, and curled up like a dried-up earthworm in the dust and dung of the narrow country road. "You broke it..."

Jenny stopped running when she saw the creek. She slowed her pace, looked side to side, then behind her, and saw that she hadn't been followed. Her ears stung, as if they'd just been boxed, but she knew they hadn't. Just his voice, taunting her with that name, made them ring. She stepped carefully into the edge of the creek and splashed water on her face. "He's a bad man, but he isn't in your life anymore. Just walk away, just walk away…"

Sudden terror hit her again. She turned back. Mr. Short was still there, lying on the ground, but now her daddy was there, too, looking over him. Her head shook back and forth, fear keeping any thoughts from forming. Back and forth, don't let bad thoughts come in. Back and forth. Keep it empty. Back and forth.

"Jenny! Jenny! Are you all right?" Wallace hollered as he ran, scared that the man on the ground—obviously suffering from a well-placed punch—had done something to hurt his Jenny. "Jenny! Jenny!"

Jenny looked up, her head still moving back and forth. She mustn't forget: words weren't allowed. Only the devil's words came out of young girls.

"Did he hurt you?" Wallace asked, holding her at arm's length, inspecting her for cuts and bruises. He turned her around and saw nothing amiss. "Look at me." Jenny's head stilled. She let him lift her face to his, her eyes not looking at him, but through him, stunned and emotionless. Wallace pulled out his silk handkerchief and wiped away the grime from around her mouth. He knew it had been spotless when they left.

"He hurt you, didn't he?"

Jenny remained mute.

"Well," he said, and wiped her mouth again to remove the last smudge, "I think you hurt him a lot more than he hurt you. At least, on the outside. Now," he locked eyes with hers, "remember, you have a mommy and a daddy now. No one is going to hurt you. And just to

48

make sure that someone doesn't hurt you when we aren't there—which I hope won't be often—I'll teach you how to fight."

One corner of Jenny's mouth turned up, and the sparkle came back to her eyes.

"And I know that you know I know how to fight. It's very important *not* to fight, but when someone tries to hurt you, and won't listen to reason, then it's all right to protect yourself. Understand?"

Jenny sighed, the other side of her mouth turning up by its self. "I understand."

"Great! Now, let's get back to the store. I think Mr. Gibson has removed Mr. Short from out front. I don't know what this town's going to do with that man. He seems to cause a lot of trouble with just his words."

"But words can hurt more than fists, huh?" Jenny asked.

"Yes, dear, they can. And the scars they leave can last a lifetime. Please, don't let anything mean people like Mr. Short say, bother you. I don't think he's right in the head. Even if he thinks he means what he says, I don't think he *knows* what he says. Does that make sense to you, or should I explain it another way?"

"It's like he's holding a rock and telling you it's an apple. Just because he says it's so, doesn't mean he's right, huh?"

"That's very right."

"So, will you tell me what a ha'penny is?"

Wallace started to ask what that had to do with anything, but knew it probably did, at least in the long run of Jenny's thinking. "A ha'penny is another way of saying half penny. That's the lowest denomination of coin minted by the British government." He realized as soon as he saw her face, that she probably didn't understand half of his words. "It's a low value coin, a piece of metal that isn't worth much."

"Oh."

Jenny knew that her daddy knew that she hadn't been to school and didn't know much, but he wanted her to learn, so if she asked him questions, it was all right. He wouldn't make her feel bad about not knowing something.

"So, when Mr. Short called me Ha'penny Jenny, he was saying I wasn't worth much?"

Wallace choked back a cough. He had wanted to laugh at the humor of the little poetic piece, but also growl at the heartlessness of the man who would call a young orphan such a cruel name. "Jenny, you are priceless. And priceless means that you are worth more than all the money in the world. "

"You mean like a whole pound sterling?" she asked, mouth and eyes wide.

"At least a hundred pounds sterling," he said. "But I wouldn't take the whole state of North Carolina in trade for you, Jenny. Not even the whole North American continent."

Wallace hugged her close, making sure she couldn't see the store. Yes, Mr. Gibson was leading Dick Short back to his house. He'd give him a few minutes to get him situated before they went back. "Come down here with me. Lets' wash up a little and get a drink before we go see Mr. Gibson again. I want to get your mother a surprise."

Jenny's eyes brightened. She knew what the surprise was. Sorta. She had heard about candy, but never had any.

It was supposed to be better than a honeycomb. Her brothers— her other brothers, who were up in heaven—once had given her part of one they had found while hunting. She smiled as she remembered how

50

much fun they all had, sucking on the little holes, chewing the wax to get the last little bits of sweetness out, licking the sticky mess off their fingers when they were done. She was sure glad she didn't have a beard like her brothers did, although they used to joke that they could still taste the sweetness days later. It was one of the best times she ever had with them. But they were with God now. He had wanted them with Him. And now they could have all the food and honey they wanted, and be warm all the time...

"Jenny, are you ready to go back to the store, or do you want to wait a little longer? Mr. Short is gone, if that makes you feel better."

Jenny sighed. Everyone was where he was supposed to be. "Okay. Let's go. Hey, how come mommy talks funny? Like the word okay. She says it means all right, but why doesn't she just say all right? Do you know what country she *really* comes from? I don't want to ask her, but I think its America. Do we live in America? I thought we lived in North Carolina. At least, that's what Grannie told me, and I know she wouldn't lie to me. So how can I live in America and North Carolina at the same time?"

"Greetings again, Mr. Gibson. Now, as far as settling for the modification of your cabinets..." Wallace didn't want to be rude and ignore Jenny's questions, but he wanted to get the business transaction finished and get back to the rest of his family. He could explain geography later, possibly even on the ride back. It would be easier to do with a map or a pen and paper, but she was sharp and would probably follow a verbal description of states within countries. Of course, he wasn't going to explain why Mommy spoke differently. He barely understood time travel—it would be easier to explain gravity to the precocious girl, and he didn't understand that, either.

"I've got salt, sugar, flour, coffee, some newer yard goods, and even a bit of that other commodity you were asking about." Mr. Gibson ended his stock list with a big grin and a glance at Jenny.

Jenny smiled back. She wanted to tell him she knew what he was talking about, even if she didn't know what the word commodity was. Maybe that was a fancy word for candy. Sometimes, it was better to say nothing, even if she didn't *have* to be quiet.

"I'll tell you what, I'd like to keep it on account, if it's all right with you."

Jenny's smile evaporated, actually turned upside down like grandpa said. Did she do something wrong?

Wallace continued, "Except I'll be taking a bit of that *commodity* back with me." He had been watching her face, and was glad to see she was positively radiant now. She was such a great guesser. She knew he was getting something for her.

Mr. Gibson reached under the counter and brought out the big apothecary jar. "Go ahead and point to which one you want," he said. "How about that big one there?"

Jenny's eyes shifted back and forth, undecided. She wanted the big piece—it would probably last her a whole year, maybe even a month. She looked up and asked her daddy, "Can we get that big one for Mommy? I know she'd like a piece of candy, and because she has to eat more so she can feed my brothers and sister—that is my new brothers, and I never had a sister, but I always wanted one, so she's my only sister ever—I'll take a smaller piece and can she have the biggest piece?"

"How about if Mr. Gibson pokes around in that jar and sees if there are two big pieces—one for you and one for Mommy?"

Jenny bounced up and down on her toes. "Ooh, ooh, really? I mean, thanks! I'd like that. And I'm sure Mommy would, too. You're the best daddy in the world. Well, I haven't met all of them, but still, I *know* you're the best daddy in the *whole* world! And thank you, too, Mr. Gibson. You're the best storekeeper in the *whole* world, too!"

Ж

The trip home was much different than the one in. Besides the fact that there was no weight in the back end of the wagon so the ride was bumpier, it was also noisier, but in a different way. The creaks, rattles, and squeaks of metal on wood, wood on wood, and wheels on rocks and packed dirt were audible now. Jenny was quiet, but in a good way. Mr. Gibson had given her a small length of new cloth to wrap around her peppermint stick.

"That's to keep your hands from getting sticky," he said. "And when you're done licking on it, you can wrap it around it to keep off dust, flies, and ants. But make sure you stop licking a few minutes before you wrap it up. Otherwise, it will be like glue and the cloth will stick to it. You don't want to have to rip it apart the next time your daddy says you can have your treat, now do you?" Jenny shook her head, her mouth wrapped around the top of her white peppermint stick. "Now, your daddy told me you're a good helper, that's why I gave you that pretty cloth. That and it matches your eyes. Get along now. I'm sure your mommy misses you. And don't forget to help her, every chance you get."

10 Please don't go

"Don't go. Please, Grandpa Jody, please don't go," begged Jenny, her eyes red and brimming, her tears almost—but not quite—spilling over.

"I'm not goin' anywhere, lass." Jody reached down, picked her up, and swung her in a tight circle. "I have to stay here and teach ye how to dance."

"Promise me you won't leave, please. Pretty please with honey and candy and flowers and sugar and please, please…"

"What's the matter, lass? I'll always be here fer ye. Yer my family—my granddaughter."

Jenny shook her head, trying to get the bloody image to go away, but it wouldn't leave. She sniffed. She couldn't tell grandpa that sometimes she 'saw' things before they happened. She'd never tell anyone *that* again. She shivered with the memory.

"Now, dinna be afeart of somethin' bad happenin' to me." Jody gave her an extra hug of reassurance. "Ye canna go through life afeart of what's on the other side of a door, or down the road, or…"

Jenny nodded rapidly, but even as he spoke the words, telling her not to worry, she saw him lying in the road, covered in blood. She squeezed him around the neck, almost choking him. "Well, *if* you have to go somewhere, be *verra* careful and don't go anywhere alone, okay?"

"All right, I promise. Now, loosen yer grip about my neck so I can show ye the proper way to dance. That is, with yer feet on the ground and yer hand on my shoulder—if it'll reach that high."

Jenny slid down his body until she was on tip toes, then reached up as high as she could with her fingertips. "I'm not tall enough yet, but I will be. Mommy said I'll grow tall and pretty if I eat my greens every day. But I can't eat too many, or I'll get a bellyache, huh?"

"Aye, lass. Too much of anythin', save lovin' yer family, is seldom a good idea. And I'll be verra careful whenever I leave yer presence. Oof! I need to stay around long enough to give ye a few more dancin' lessons, at least. Yer next partner's feet may nae be as tough as mine."

Jenny looked up at him again, squinting hard. Maybe he'd be okay now that he promised not to be alone.

But maybe not.

The sadness was still there.

But now there was hope. And help.

Someone else was coming to their home, maybe next month, maybe next week.

And maybe he'd bring a big sister for her, too.

Ж‌Ж‌Ж

The End

Ha'penny Jenny

Book One and a half (novella)

The Fairies Saga

More adventures follow in

Aye, I am a Fairy

Book Two in the series

The Fairies Saga

To find out how Jenny became a member of the family, read

Naked in the Winter Wind

Book One in the series

The Fairies Saga

Thanks, in no particular order

Thank you, Elaine Boyle, editor and historian, for your gentle guidance and suggestions. I know I'm frustrating, insisting on sourdough products and calling 18th century parents Mommy and Daddy, but Evie's 21st century leanings are tough—as tough as her determination.

Thanks, Marty Haviland, the world's greatest husband, for your support and patience…and for taking me out to dinner when I'm too tired to cook.

Thanks, Diana Gabaldon, for your words of encouragement to write and for creating the *Outlander* series, the inspiration for the *Lost* series that my Sarah and Jody are 'from.'

Thanks, Kim Killion and Hot Damn Designs, for the brilliant cover (and Jenny's cute dress) you created.

Thanks, Amazon and CreateSpace, for all the tools you provide free of charge to help authors and artists bring their work to others. Publishing made easy. Double thanks.

Thanks, Leatherman Tool Company, for having such great multitools that they're mentioned by brand name by my former Alaskans.

Cast of Characters

Captain Atholl MacLeod ~ evil Redcoat officer who had previously attacked Jenny

Clayton ~ Jenny's deceased brother—was crude and crass

Clyde ~ Jenny's deceased brother—was crude and crass

Evie ~ 20th century born older woman, transported back to 18th century, has amnesia, now in young body due to an overdose of Fountain of Youth Water. Jenny's mother

Ian Kincaid ~ 18th century backwoodsman, aka Starwalker

Jenny ~ once orphaned preadolescent girl

Jody Pomeroy ~ family patriarch, Jenny's adopted grandfather

Jose' ~ Spanish emigrant, Julian's partner

Julian Hart ~ Wallace's stepfather, Jenny's other grandfather

Leah ~ 21st century daughter of Evie

Mr. Gibson ~ 18th century storekeeper

Mrs. Short ~ Jenny's former 'caretaker'

Richard 'Dick' Short ~ local troublemaker, 18th century

Sarah Pomeroy ~ Jody's wife, 20th century-born time traveler, healer, living in 18th century, Jenny's grannie

Wallace ~ 18th century British soldier, Julian's stepson, Jenny's father

Wren, Leo, Judah ~ Evie's six-week-old infants

www.ingramcontent.com/pod-product-compliance
Lightning Source LLC
Chambersburg PA
CBHW071237170626
46809CB00008BA/3094